Written by Rosie Greening.
Illustrated by Stuart Lynch.

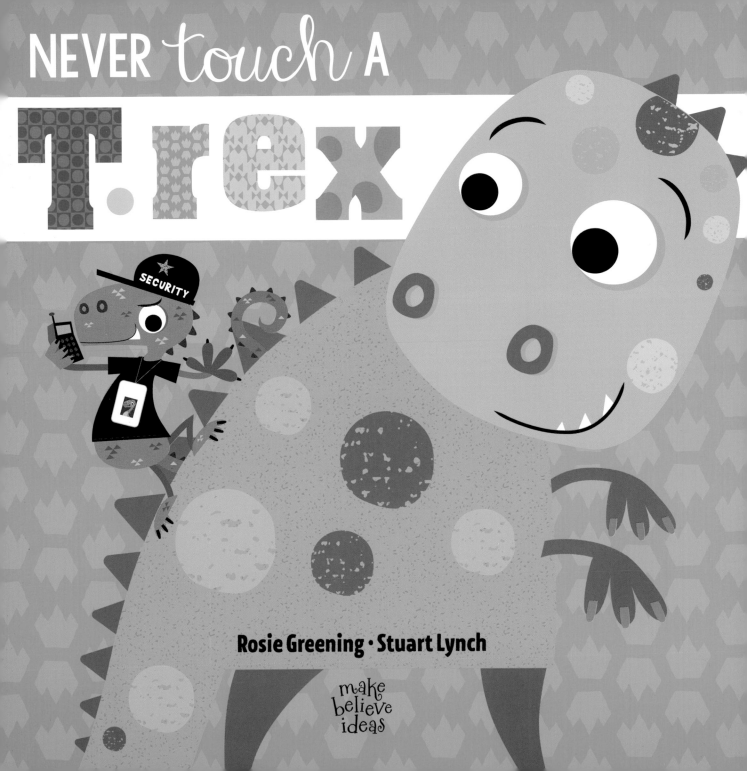

# NEVER *touch* A
# T. rex

**Rosie Greening · Stuart Lynch**

*make believe ideas*

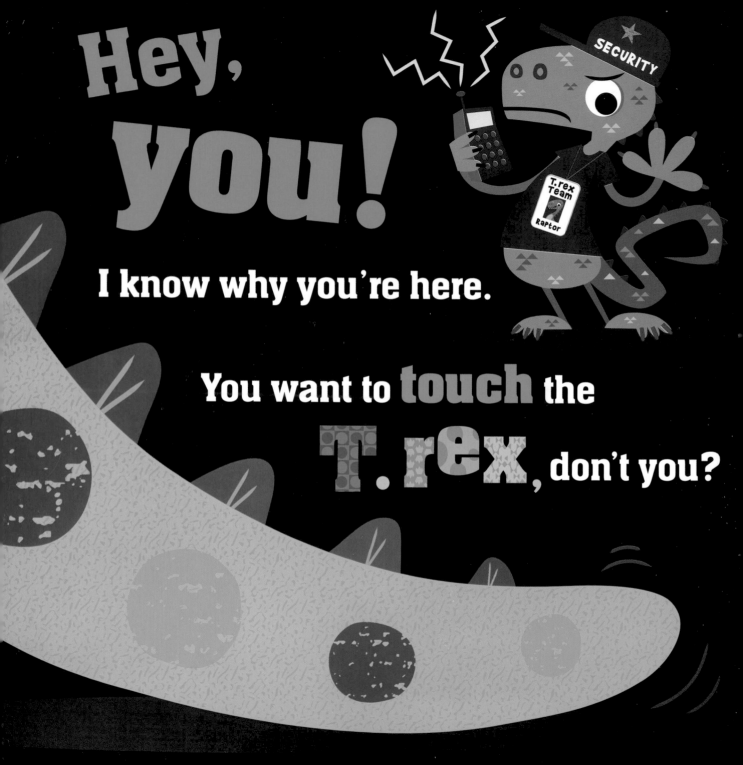

# WELL YOU CAN'T.

Here's the **rule:**

You must never touch a T. rex, unless you . . .

. . . point to your nose.

**There's no way you can point to your nose. Just you try!**

Okay, this is the **real** rule. You must **never** touch a  **T. rex**, unless you . . .

**. . . POINT to your nose**

**and TOUCH your toes!**

Ha! Try those if you think you're so clever.

# Okay, genius.

## The actual rule is this:

Never touch a T. rex,

unless you . . .

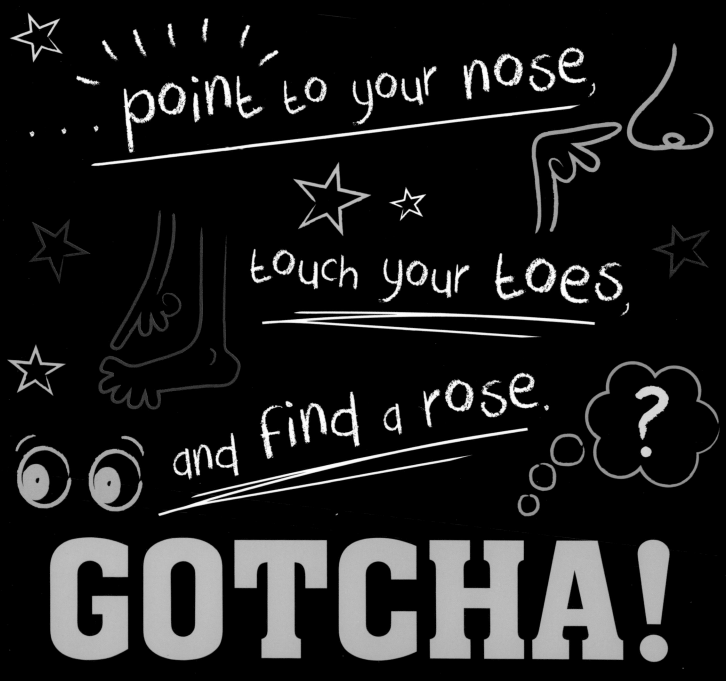

 You won't find a **rose** on this page.

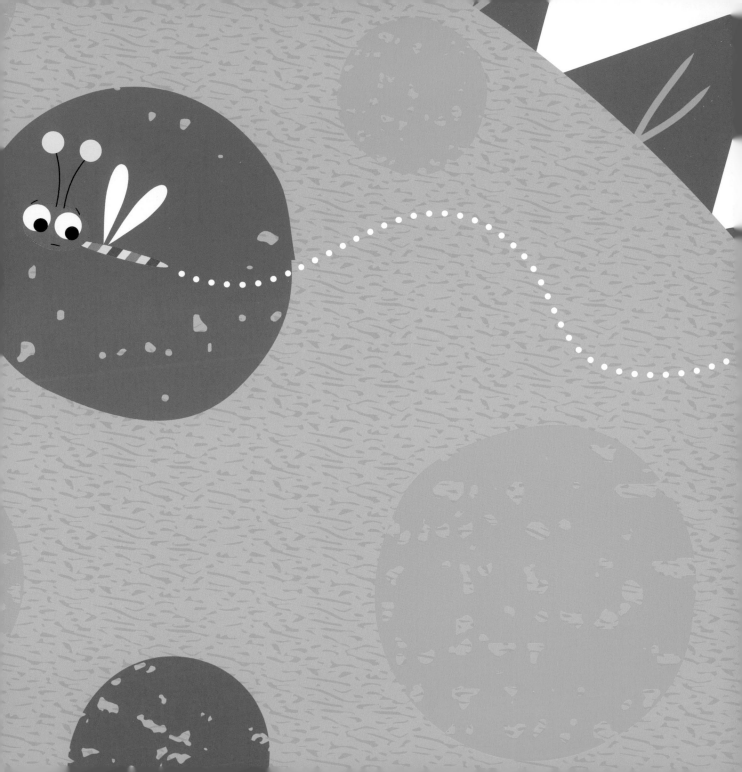

touch **your** toes,

find a rose,

and shout,

"Banana!"

# Have you done this before?

It's **lucky** I have a plan . . .

You must never touch a **T. rex,**
unless you . . . .

find
a rose,

I COUNT 2
to three, 3

touch
your toes,

Wave
at me,

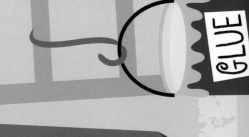

GLUE

. . . point
to your
nose,

Shout, "BANANA!"

meow
like a cat,
FLAP
like a
BAT,
SECURITY
T.rex
Team
Raptor
sing HIGH,
then low,
SAAAAAAAY
SOOOMETHIIIIIING
SLOOOOOWWWW . . .

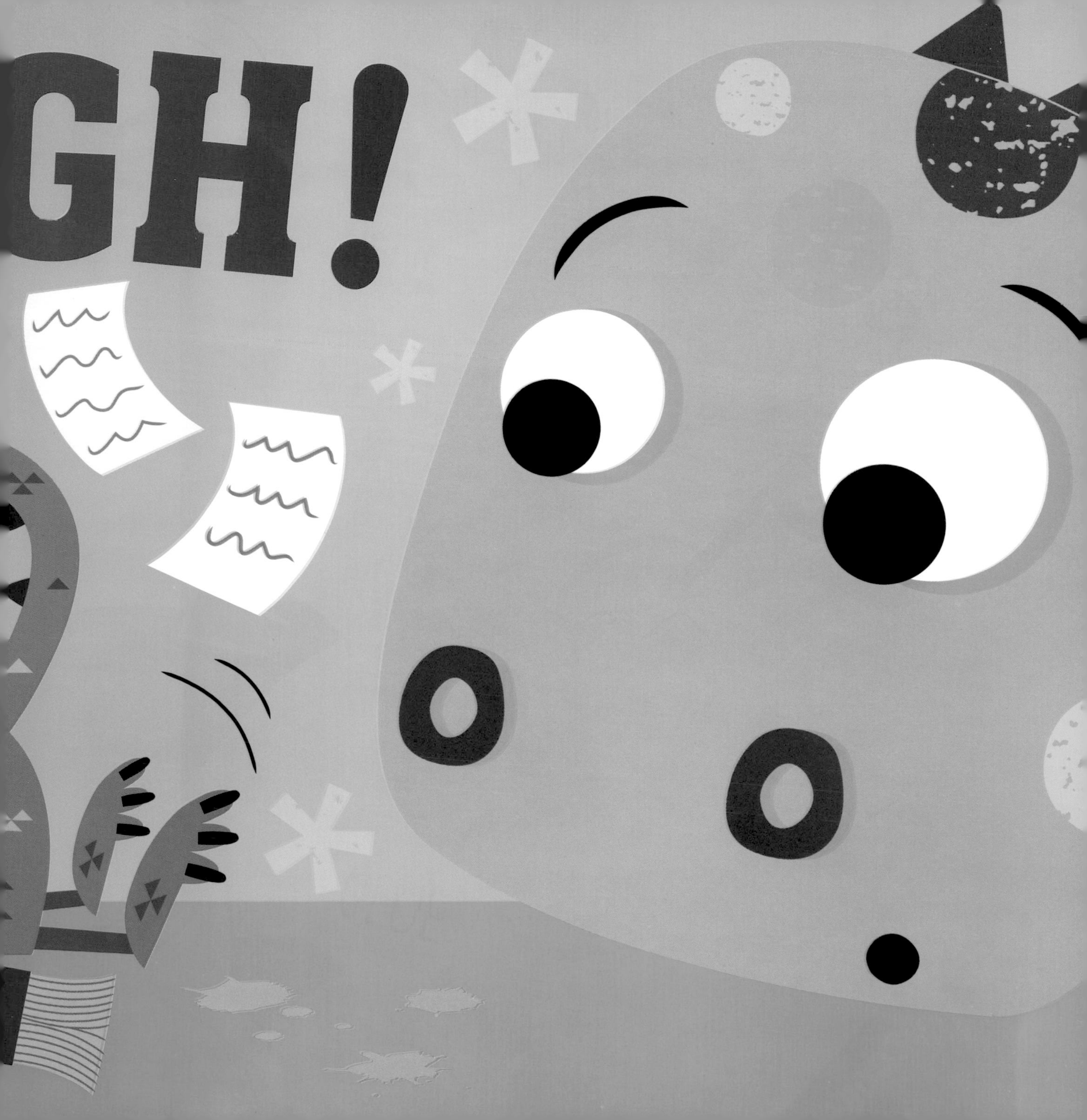
GH!

**"HELLO!**

**Sorry** about the guard.

There's really only **one** rule you need to know.

You must **never** touch a T. rex, unless you . . .

ASK POLITELY.

Go on, **give it a try!**"

"How **nice** and **polite** you are!

# OF COURSE
# YOU CAN!"

**Okay,** okay.

You're brighter than I thought.
But I've got one more rule for you:

**DON'T CLOSE**
this book!

THE END